!y

Nalle Windahl

The M3rqrie series

Second book

First edition

Förlag: BoD – Books on Demand, Stockholm, Sverige
Tryck: BoD – Books on Demand, Norderstedt, Tyskland

ISBN: 978-91-8027-005-2

This book is meant as entertainment only. None of the organizations or used components are real, only fiction.

Part I

Lost

Waking up from the best nightmare ever

Did you wake up? Did you find your white rabbit? Did it lead you somewhere unexpected?

Mine did. I found the N3v3r!and. I lived my dream. No, better than my dream! I got everything I ever dared to wish for. But it was a dream. And the price tag was just too high. I could not live with myself knowing the things I found out. I could not be part of it.

I woke up, from the best dream that I've ever had, but it turned into a nightmare. And the worst part is that the nightmare remained even after I woke up.

My life before finding N3v3r!and was not exactly prime time, but it was a good, stable and independent life. Far away from the real action. Far away from the "real" world, only circling like a fish in the deep pond of the dark web. But I knew that life was more than that, I knew that the world was more than that. My rabbit opened my eyes. And as mr. Andersson in the Matrix, I saw the entire world in a different light. And just like mr. Andersson, I cannot undo the experience. I woke up. Didn't like what I saw. I left. I started to resist and fight. I was naive. For a little while I really thought I could bring down the N3v3r!and on my own. Turned out I could not. Turned out many had tried before me. They could not either. But others had tried. That was good news for me.

But again, let's start at the beginning, this new beginning that followed after leaving the N3v3r!and.

Lone Wolf

Have you seen Rambo - first blood part 2? That was my first contact with both the character John Rambo, and with the actor Sylverster Stallone.

The younger me, also feeling like an outsider, was greatly inspired by the absolutely amazing things one person could do. Rambo's field name Lone Wolf, it was my first identity on the web. And after leaving the N3v3r!and, knowing I needed to disappear and once again break all bonds with the world as I knew it, I mentally saw myself being reborn as the Lone Wolf yet again.

I needed to take on the N3v3r!and alone and try to inflict them as much damage as I possibly could, hopefully even bring it down. *Somehow, somewhere* as Muddhedd put it in a title (freely interpreted).

My enemy, as I knew it, was located in London. Thus, after walking out on my life, only telling Bella, I stayed in London, but hidden. I thought.

Turns out that it is hard to hide from the N3v3r!and. Especially in their own backyard.

The big pile of money I had gotten from my old life had slowly grown from my time as a well paid consultant at Barrie IT, and I knew that money would not be a problem for a while, but I figured that I needed to find a new way to make money. But I also knew that the old ways that I had used before finding the N3v3r!and would be impossible to go back to, they would find me right away.

And I kind of figured that me walking out on them would not be very appreciated.

Now, for being a good hacker, and a paranoid person, I was pretty stupid. And I am not saying anything to defend my poor choices, nor the lack of clear thinking, but when I left, it was a big loss for me as a person. Clouded judgment had put me in a tricky place, both in walking in the cut path put in front of me by the N3v3r!and, and breaking my own rules and promises to myself and connected to Bella, both emotionally, mentally and physically. First getting the life that I always secretly had dreamed of, then having to choose to leave it all behind, especially Bella.

The entire situation made me rush down the stress cone without thinking clearly, and the more I rushed, forcing myself to act, while I still could, the worse it got. It was like the situation put blinders on me, leaving me with a very slim field of view, and a single minded way to think. Which, according to me, is a good way to set yourself up for failure before you even start.

The new operation

I rushed into a new operation. I first dropped off the grid (I thought) by physically leaving the known parts of London, hiding out in the outskirts. I left everything behind, except a bag of clothes, my phone and my computer. Both the phone and computer were big mistakes to keep. Both were red flagged by the N3v3r!and as soon as I stopped showing up.

I knew they had one of my bank accounts since I got pay checks from them, but I honestly believed that they did not have a list of all my accounts. Thus, fully aware that they would be able to track each and every economic transaction connected to my credit cards, I figured I needed old fashioned real money to get my way around. I made a large withdrawal from one of my accounts and got as much cash as I dared carrying around with me, everywhere I went. Knowing cash is untraceable. Or cash is king, as some say. Up until now, I had really never thought about it, but it turns out that cash is not king, not by far. But it took me a while to discover that.

Once I had a place to stay, fairly good ways to finance it, it was time to go to work. The new operation, as I imagined it, was to break the 3ld3rs by exposing them in any way I could.

I figured that there had to be dirt on them, and I needed to find it and report it to the right authority. I hoped to be able to present very interesting and well supported cases to any investigator, perhaps, if I was lucky, to several. Economic, tax-related, criminal, bribery, whatever I could dig up.

Once the 3ld3rs has fallen, I would try to infiltrate the emergency backup protocol to gain access and control of the surrounding cells, leaving them in my command.

At the time, it seemed like a solid and simple enough plan, and I honestly believed it would work. Naiv and wrong. It was one of the quickest and most embarrassing failures in my life.

The failure

I did not have the inside access to the Barrie IT infrastructure anymore, and even at that point, despite my strange blind spots, I realized that I could not use that method to get the information I wanted. So, using public systems, still from my own computer, I traced the 3ld3rs to find out their real names and private addresses. But I only managed to find the true identity of P@nm@n when an unwelcome window popped up on my screen. A terminal window with the words "Knock, knock…"

It was another Matrix reference. And I immediately realized that my computer was compromised. I closed the lid at once and ran out of the café I was currently at, and took the shortest way to the Thames and threw it in the water. I needed to get my hands on new gear.

My initial reaction was to go to the nearest media store to get a new laptop, and as I was about to enter, my phone vibrated in my pocket. It was an incoming text.

"I hear they have a really good deal on the Lenovo Yoga's here…"

I stopped in the middle of my step, in the middle of the door, almost blocking the other customers on the way in or out.

They were watching me. They knew exactly where I was, and what I was doing. I turned around, saw a McDonald's restaurant and went in there, hoping to find a microwave that parents could use to heat food for their babies. They did. And

I put my phone in there, pushed start, and the lightshow inside confirmed to me that it had been rendered completely useless.

Now I was digitally disconnected from the world. Untraceable. I thought.

A quick change of clothes, hood up and a pair of freshly stolen sunglasses, I exited and blended in with the crowd.

I thought I could shake them and lose them. Turned out I didn't. But they made me believe it for the time being.

It took a few days to find and buy a preowned computer and an old school mobile phone with 4G-capacity and cable attachment to the computer. Reinstalling the computer and getting my basic toolkit on it took no time at all, and I felt like I was back in business. And this time I made sure to add a few extra layers of paranoia security to prevent further surprises.

I could finish what I had started, without any more incidents. Of course I was extra careful on each step and took time to carefully hide my traces.

I also acquired a few gadgets and built me a few discreet bugging devices, old school with radio transmitters. So I could install a recorder with radio receivers in close proximity and get the proof I needed.

My first target, just happening to be the closest, was H0kr. As I bypassed the apartment security, again with various gadgets that I had acquired and repurposed, I went inside to install the bugging devices. But I had not more than entered the hallway inside the door when I heard the TV start in a nearby room. It scared the hell out of me, since I was convinced that nobody was home. At first I did not get it, but after a few seconds, when the chock eased off, I realized that it was a movie playing, but not any random movie, it was Star Wars - Rogue One. A coincidence or a subtle message to me?

Then the stereo started, playing the first few seconds of the Queen song "Don't stop me", then skipped track to "Under pressure" and after a few seconds "I want to break free", then "Killer Queen" followed by "We will rock you", then "Another one bitest the dust" and lastly "We are the Champions"... at that point I knew they were on to me and sending me messages through one of my favorite groups. And as I turned to the door to get out, they skipped to the last song I heard, "The show must go on"...

Lost and found

I felt lost. And I felt like I had lost. This enemy was too powerful and I had clearly underestimated them.

As I thought about how they had tracked me I remembered the facial recognition software and the enhancements I had helped install and develop. This meant that I could not go anywhere in London where there was a camera. Which basically was everywhere. This would be true for any other place as well, if not now than in a reasonably nearby timeframe as the Barrie IT and the N3v3r!and expanded their system integrations.

I needed to get lost, for real. But I had nowhere to go. I felt beaten. Check mate. The end of the game and the end of the road. My only option was to surrender. But again, I was wrong.

As I randomly flead through the streets of London, slowly moving outwards from the center, I got the feeling I was followed. Now I have followed people before, at a distance, but being followed was a whole new experience, and not a pleasant one either.

In panic, I headed for the nearest train station and boarded a train bound for Brighton. As the train left the station and I had not gotten any glimpse of my tail, I tried to slow down my heavily beating heart and my breath to get to a state of mind where I could think clearly.

And after a few stops down south, I had calmed myself down just enough to be able to think. That's when it happened. A man entered the cart I was sitting in, looked around, spotted me and headed right towards me, not taking his eyes from me or even blinking.

He sat down right next to me without asking if the seat was taken.

I felt the panic in me rise in no time, and I wished I had some kind of weapon to defend myself with.

He spoke to me in a low voice that I barely could hear, and probably no one else around either. He had an accent, but I could not place it at once.

"M3rqrie. I believe we have a common enemy. I will get off at the next station. If you decide to trust me, just follow me, but don't walk with me, keep a distance of at least 10 meters at all times. I'll take you to a safe place where we can talk. Do not make any attempt to talk to me here or on the way. I'll let you know when it is safe to speak. Leave your computer and phone here."

Then he took out a book and started to read and ignored me completely. In a tunnel where it was pitch black outside the window, there was a distorted reflection in the window. I caught a glimpse of the title of the book he was reading. It was "Peter Pan".

I decided to trust him. For the time being.

Safe House

As he said, when the train slowed down before reaching the next station, he rose from his seat and headed for the doors. I waited a little, honestly, I was hesitating. A million thoughts ran through my head. But my gut feeling still said trust him, so I got up from my seat and followed him at a distance.

He exited the station and walked towards a bus station. Stood there waiting for a bus. So, I followed his example, trying not to look at him too much. But it was hard, my head kept turning in his direction, and as it did, I tried to divert my eyes elsewhere, so I must have read the ads on the bus stop walls about 256 times while we waited.

He seemed indifferent about just about everything and had a kind of detached autopilot while waiting. Not in the ordinary commuters way who enters their own world of thoughts, but almost as if he was in standby mode and was unpresent.

I have no idea how long we waited, but we got on the second bus that departed from the bus stop, and I had to stand because the bus was so crowded. The man had taken a seat at the back and was reading in his book again. Either he enjoyed the book, or at least actually read it, or he was a really good actor. But I could not believe it was a coincidence that it was Peter Pan. Of all books in the world he had to choose from when intercepting me. No, it had to be a deliberate choice. And a kind of signal.

After a few stops the bus had emptied enough for me to find a seat. But there were no seats available except for seats with the back turned towards the man, which would make me unaware if he got off somewhere. And I knew I could not turn around and peek at him before each stop. Luckily, there was a seat right behind the driver's seat, and behind the driver, separating him from all the travelers, there was a black glass wall, partially covered with ads. But the uncluttered glass spaces made a pretty good mirror, giving me an opportunity to peek at the man and keep a close tab on him, without looking directly at him.

The further the bus went, the emptier it got, and it seemed like the bus only emptied, without taking on any new passengers. After a while there were only three people left on the bus, not counting the driver. And it seemed like the ride kept on forever.

Then, the driver announced that the next stop was the end of the line, and that we all needed to get off.

We did, and the other passenger went off in one direction, the man in another, so it was kind of hard to act like I was not following him.

After a few blocks he rounded a corner to an old house, and I had to hurry to the corner, afraid that I might lose him. And at the same time, I thought that this would be a perfect place for an ambush. The thought sent chills down my spine, but my gut feeling still said that I needed to trust him.

As I arrived at the corner, I was just in time to see him walking down a stair and enter a door that led to the basement of the house. He did not look back to see if I had seen him, he just went inside and the door shut behind him.

!y

I arrived at the top of the stairs the man had just used to go down to the door. And when I saw the door I stopped in the middle of my step.

On the door, handwritten with red paint, was an exclamation mark followed by the letter y. !y

What was this? A subdivision of N3v3r!and? An enemy to the N3v3r!and? A different team in the same game? Perhaps a competitor to the N3v3r!and? Was this a kind of recruitment or a debrief session to get me to give up everything I know about the N3v3r!and? And if so, to what end?

A part of me wanted to turn around and go away. Another part of me was curious as to what was behind that door. And when I reasoned with logic, I could really not see any other option than to go through that door to the unknown behind it. (By the way, Unknown - another Muddhedd release!) Mostly because I had no idea of where else I could go in this situation.

It was with a pounding heart that I took the steps down the stairs to the door. And I stood with my hand on the handle a while before I decided to open the door. I remember that I held my breath as I opened it and walked through.

On the other side of the door was a small corridor. The floor was raw concrete and the walls were painted in a horrible orange color. Here and there the paint was flaking…

"…my make-up may be flaking, but my smile still stays on…"

The light was poor since there was only a lonely naked lightbulb on one side. It was attached directly to the electrical wiring and two cables were visible sticking out of the wall. Electrical safety hazard.

I slowly took a few steps towards the end of the corridor. There were no doors on either side, the only one I could see was at the far end. It was not entirely closed, and I assumed that the man was waiting for me behind it.

It felt like it took forever to reach the door, but in reality I believe it was just a matter of seconds. But I could almost not hear any other sounds than my own heartbeat pounding so loud that I thought my chest would explode, taking my head with it.

Security control

As I slowly pushed the door open, the room behind it was revealed bit by bit. I could not really piece together what I saw until the door was fully open and I could take in the whole picture. Sure enough the man was waiting for me, and he made it a complete picture. And I could not help but let a laugh slip out.

The room looked like a security check at an airport, and the man was holding a sweeper that he almost instantly started scanning my body with.

I drew my breath to say something, but he gave me a quick glance and shook his head and continued his sweep. After a while, he seemed pleased and gestured at me to pass through a security gate. Looked almost like the ones they had at Barrie IT, perhaps an older model. It did not make a sound. Obviously it approved of me passing through. As I waited on the other side of the gate, the man swept himself with the scanner, and as he was satisfied he passed through the gate as well.

He signed for me to move along and follow a tiny corridor that seemed to take us back towards the door we came in through, but on the other side of the orange wall. This corridor was much more narrow, and even if I am not big, I had to keep my arms close to my sides to keep from bumping into the walls. I felt a little claustrophobic, and kept on moving forward as quickly as I possibly could, but I couldn't help but wonder if the man behind me had to twist his upper body to fit through here. His steps were close behind me, so either way I had to keep moving.

Entering the cage

At the end of the corridor, near what I assumed was the outer wall, there was another sharp turn and we came to a dead end where the path to continue was blocked by a metal gate that led to some sort of cage.

Directly behind the locked gate was a step up on the cage floor. The floor, the walls and the roof were all made of a kind of metal net. This became stranger and stranger, and I did not know what to expect anymore. Just tag along for the ride and see where it took me.

The man reached past me and put his hand on a biometric scanner next to the gate. As the scan was completed, there was a buzzing sound which sounded as if it came from an old and big motorized lock, or perhaps several, and the gate swung open with a squeaky sound.

We entered the cage, and the man pulled a liver inside the gate, who slowly closed again, and once the motorized locks had stopped their synchronized odd song, he turned towards me and nodded.

"Now, M3rqrie, we can talk, please continue further down and take a right around the corner."

When I was allowed to talk, I could not think of anything to say, not right away anyway. Walking on the strange net floor was a strange feeling. It was not completely solid, it sagged a little for each step.

After the corner was another long narrow corridor and after that a big windowless room, still encased in this odd metallic net.

In the far end of the room, there was a big tech rigg with various screens and keyboards. On the right was a worn down sofa, and on the left a table with two chairs and a kitchen cabinet with some kitchen appliances.

He gestured towards the sofa. And I sat down between two worn pillows and a blanket.

Paranoia

"Introductions perhaps?" he asked me, as he sat down on one of the chairs by the tech rig.

I nodded.

"Obviously, I know you are M3rqrie. That much I have already shared with you. As for me, I'm Even. Real name Ivan. But I was renamed when I left the N3v3r!and and wanted to get even with them."

As he spoke, and mentioned his real name, I could place his accent. Russian.

"I am part of the network !y (not why), but some call us Ly (lie). As you are probably already aware, truth is a perspective, thus, lies are also a perspective, but a more complicated one."

He paused for a while, to give me an opportunity to say something, but I didn't.

"As you might guess, I know about the N3v3r!and, and I know that you are a part of it, or were, if I assume correctly. My first question to you is simple: do you see yourself as an enemy of the N3v3r!and or a refugee from it?"

Without hesitation, my answer came quickly. "Enemy."

"Thought so! We share your point of view. We do also consider them enemy. Perhaps for the same reason, perhaps not, time will tell. My second question is related to your answer; are you willing to fight them?"

Again, a quick answer, but this time I just nodded.

"Good. Now, before I continue. Do you know where we are?"

I shook my head.

"This is one of our safe houses. We do not have many, but this is the closest we have to London. It is not only a safe house, it doubles as our operation center in the UK. We're too close to the dragon here, which is why we keep an extra low profile.. Each safe house is located inside a Faraday cage, no signals can get in or out, except the ones we choose. The scanners that you passed when entering, is mandatory to make sure that no bugs are brought here. Intentionally or unintentionally. As you probably understand, we are a bit paranoid. But it has worked out for us so far, and we will continue on that path."

"When you say we, who do you mean?" I had to ask. A name does not give away much, nor that they considered the N3v3r!and enemies, even if it was good news. Possible allies.

Consultant

"Long answer. But the short version would be that we are a balancing force. As the N3v3r!and take action, we make counter actions. But we do not just balance the N3v3r!and, but they are on our top priority list. We do not work on the public arena, we stay away from the shadows. We stay here in the sewers. Here we can see what happens, what other flushes down. We see the results. We don't ask why, we just see, then act."

"Not why, I get it! Cleaver! And now you are recruiting me, since I left the N3v3r!and and you want to see if I am willing to work for you?"

"Don't flatter yourself! We are not recruiting, not at the moment anyway, but yes. We want something from you, and we are willing to offer you some protection during a temporary alliance. From our perspective you would be like a consultant."

"A consultant? Then what?"

"Don't know, we do not plan that far ahead. We see, we react."

"Not why! I get it! What is it that you want from me?"

"Also long story."

"Well, I'm not in a hurry, I kind of have nowhere else to go, and nowhere else to be, so for now, I'm stuck with you, here in this cage, for as long as you decide. Please take your time."

"Alright. Do you know why we are in this 'cage'?"

"No. You said Faraday cage, so I assume this is shielded from all kinds of electromagnetic waves. But from the looks of this place I'd say that it is not military grade, almost looks homemade."

"Bah, ignorant fool. These are Russian quality components. And you are wrong. We are not shielded from everything. When you were recruited. At the Guy Fawkes place. Did the computer have any other cables attached to it, other than the power cable?"

"No, not that I recall…"

"No network interface, no WiFi, no BlueTooth device?"

"No, not that I could see from the short time period that I had there…"

"And I assume that you got contacted straight after exiting the building, while the alarm still sounded?"

"Just about, yes!"

"How do you think they managed to do that?"

New perspectives

"I don't know, perhaps they have someone on the inside, in the security team maybe. Haven't really thought about it."

"Did you think about why it was an old terminal, old screen and an old mechanical keyboard?"

"No. Have not given it much thought."

"And if I ask you to think about it now, what conclusions can you draw?"

I thought for a while. They had built this cage for a reason. There was a reason for the bug-sweeping.

"Because they had the room bugged somehow?"

"Yes, in two ways. That is why we are sitting in this cage. What two ways could it be?"

"The first would be sound. And perhaps an algorithm that can identify keystrokes from the keyboard?"

"Yes, correct, that is one of two reasons. The KGB developed a way to spy on the Americans back when everybody still used typewriters. They hid microphones and recorded the typing. Then, a specialist would identify the type of typewriter, and listen to the recording to decipher what keys were used and in what order. Using this method, the KGB got hold of important intel for many years. The technology later replaced human analysts."

"Then I guess that the second reason would be of the same type, the electromagnetic field surrounding the Cathode Ray Tubes in the screens?"

"Correct. Both methods are used by the N3v3r!and to automatically log any usage of that computer and send automated information to the 3ld3rs. They get the information without the need to physically access the information on the computer."

"That explains a lot."

"Which is why we are sitting in this cage. Each of our locations are shielded the same. I must say I'm impressed. I did not think you would figure it out. Even though your file says you are smart and have a big experience with tech."

"Why does the !y have a file on me?"

"We don't, the N3v3r!and does."

Getting answers

"But why do you have access to that information?"

"Because they have not told you everything."

"Then fill in the blanks for me."

"Alright. The N3v3r!and are a global movement, right?"

"Right!"

"Does it make sense that they would have their offline information securely stored in one place only? Without backup?"

"No! Not really!"

"So, just to prove to you that we have access to the information, I can share with you that they have classified you as a rogue operator, with low probability to cause them any damage, and with a termination at the N3v3r!and, even if you would choose to return?"

"What does that information prove? You could have made it up just now…" I was a bit hurt by what he said.

"Then I can share details that they started Rogue One on the TV when you were inside H0kr's apartment, and that they played the intros to various Queen songs. Do you want me to name what songs and in what order?"

My jaws dropped. How did he know this?

"I take your reaction as a no. And I will explain how we have the information. First, their infrastructure. As you probably know from working with the Happy Roger, there are no landlines to or from the site, except for the diods you yourself have installed. Correct?"

"As far as I know, yes!"

"Well, as I said earlier, the N3v3r!and are a global movement, they have more places like the Happy Roger. One in London, one in New York, and others in Hong Kong, Perth and believe it or not, one in Iceland. All connected to each other, sharing information through satellite networks. All sites synchronized and acting as off site backups for each other."

Made total sense.

"And, just so happens, satellites are our area of expertise."

The satellite network

What he told me next, I could almost not believe.

They had hijacked an old Soviet satellite network and used it as their communication with the outside world. The Soviet did not want to publicly admit that they had lost control of an entire satellite network, and were afraid that the !y would take control of a more modern satellite network, they kind of just let them have it. But since it was a global network, owned by the Russians these days, it was part of the backup communications protocols for all international space corporations. Alongside with european and american satellite networks. That provided the !y with backdoors to almost all active satellite networks, including the one that the N3v3r!and used as a synchronization service for their 'offline' sites.

He made a gesture towards the operation stations behind him.

"This is what we use to connect to our network. We have installed modern encryption, so our bandwidth is highly limited. About 300 Baud."

"What?! 300 Baud? You are joking? That would be about 30 characters per second?!"

"Yes. Sounds about right. Which is why we need to be exact and know exactly what we send and why. Miscalculations can send feedback loops within the network, and it can take several weeks to regain access and break through the data storms."

"How do you even get something done with only 30 characters per second? I mean, I typically send package-bursts that are 10000 times bigger, and I send huge amounts of those each second. Does not make sense with only 300 Baud."

"Sense or no sense, it is what it is, we adapt to it. We don't ask why, we just do with what we have. It has kept us creative. Wait until you hear about the rest of the infrastructure."

"Please do share."

The botnets

"At our disposal, we have a very competent IoT-hacker. We call him Jack Reacher, after the movie! He is a complete asshole and equally brilliant, but he is Jackpot for us, which is the Jack part, and the Reacher part is that he is because he is both the Preacher and the Breecher, depending on what mood he is in... When he preaches, there is no stopping him, and our ears go numb after a while, and when he is in breecher-mode, well, also unstoppable."

"What do you mean by IoT-hacker?"

"Well, you know like most Unix, Linux and the entire Open Source community uses standardized libraries? The same for IoT-devices. Except there is a big difference. Here is mostly one person who has contributed to the code in almost every part of the libraries. Our Jack. And besides the functionality and security layers, he has also added a few extra features, like backdoors we can use."

"Impressive."

"Not when you hear why."

"Alright, why?"

"Because he is an asshole, balls to bones, mostly balls... he is fixated on porn, and his obsession has driven him to IoT so he can hijack cameras to get nudes from just about anybody he wants. He has also extended his vast knowledge to other devices that contain cameras, like computers, phones and pads. And of course home security systems. The upside for us is that we can use these backdoors to get access to memory, CPU power and storage, but only a tiny fraction of what the devices can manage, so we can use it undetected. And since it is mostly IoT devices, the market is exploding with things, giving us more and more resources to use. Which makes our botnets grow exponentially."

"Perv! How can you even work with someone like that?"

"Well, let's just say we need him. And with we I really mean Virtual. Our server guy. He has written an operating system that can utilize all available ram, CPU and storage and use it to create dynamic accessible virtual machines. Each operation we have online is launched from one of the dynamic machines, and when its task is performed, it vanishes, and does not leave any trace."

"OK, so from what I have heard so far, there is the perv, Virtual, and I've met you, what's your function?"

"I'm a kind of intel officer. I make sure we have access to the information and plan our online activity and divert our resources to the right tasks."

The three man army

"Ok, so that's three, how many are you in total?"

"Three."

"What? Only three?"

"Yup! Only three, a holy trinity. And as I said before, we do not recruit. Occasionally use consultants like yourself when we have the need."

"And exactly what operations are you performing?"

"It varies, but let's just say that we are in the information balancing business. When the balance is interrupted, by the N3v3r!and or any other part, we share or direct information to restore the balance."

"And what balance would that be?"

"Well, freedom of choice. Keeping people out of other people's business. Preventing governments or companies from becoming too powerful or limiting people too much."

"And the three of you pull this off?"

"So far."

"And exactly is it you want from me?"

"Let's start with a statement. You've made a big mistake and a big mess, not for us, but for a lot of others like us that prefer to remain undetected."

"How so?"

"Your integration and algorithms to the face recognition softwares. You've just handed the N3v3r!and a completely new toolset, one that gives them the advantage for the next five years or so."

"Maybe."

"No, not maybe, that's the cold fact. And what you do not know is that they also have access to next gen tech that they are currently working on to integrate as well."

"What would that be?"

"Behavior algorithms. Monitor everything, movement, what you eat, expressions on your face, what you watch on TV, when you wake up or go to bed. As long as you keep doing what you normally do, nothing happens. But as soon as something is changed in your behavior, you can be targeted for further investigation, based on what criteria you set up. Until you entered the N3v3r!and, the only thing they could apply this tech to was GPS-tracking and so on, but now, with your brilliant work they have the keys to almost every available public camera and all still and moving images of social media feeds. Gives a huge base of data to apply that algorithm to."

The request

"So you would like me to give you the code?"

"Yes and no. If we only wanted the code, we could take it from the N3v3r!and, we would like you to work with Reacher to implement your thinking and functions in his software."

"Giving the perv further access to peek at people?"

"Undoubtedly he would make use of it, yes. Now he is limited in extracting material that humans can do in realtime from the captured content and feeds. I am sure he would like to automate and get less overhead data."

"Now why would I do that?"

"Two reasons. One, currently, you have nowhere to go, nowhere to hide. You would not last long, given the tool you yourself have given them. Two, it looks to me as if you would like to bring them down. Even if we do not have the exact same goal, we are interested in keeping the balance, and not let them have the upper hand they currently got, thanks to you."

"You are playing on my guilt and my current predicament in a tight situation. What's in it for me?"

"The deal is divided in two parts. The first part is to assist Reacher. This will get you safe passage out of England, to another secure site with an operationcenter. You'll stay there for as long as the work demands, and then you are free to go.

We can help you on the first part of the journey, but then you are on your own."

"That does not sound like I am getting much out of the first part of the deal, as where you will gain significantly."

"The reward is mostly a cleaner conscience. Knowing you have helped restore the balance that you've just interrupted to the favor of your own enemies."

"And the second part?"

"Well, from the second part you will gain significantly more. We can make you rich beyond what you've ever could dream of. Set you up with connections to take you anywhere in the world, undetected, untraceable, not only for you, but perhaps for someone you care about as well? You could disappear from this world entirely, and would never have to resurface for any reason and spend the remainder of your life in luxury and abundance."

"Now, what would you like from me to get all that?"

"The sweeper code."

"Even if it is not completely done?"

"You'll need to complete it."

"Why would I agree to that and give you that tool?"

"Again, two reasons. The N3v3r!and is implementing it, and we would like to have access to a similar tool to keep the balance. But the biggest reason being for your own safety."

"How so?"

"Well, the N3v3r!and have gathered a lot of information and proof on you, and can easily set you up for a long time in jail in a number of countries. We have access to this information, I can show it to you."

"So, you want to use this to black mail me into cooperation?"

"Not at all, we have no incitament to use this information, they do, and I believe that they will not hesitate to use it."

"And once you get the sweeper code, you can make that information disappear?"

"Yes, along with any traces of you, if you like…"

The personal advice

"Sounds to me like I do not have much choice…"

"Oh, believe me, there are always choices… sadly, in your situation, I've seen too many that have chosen to not be able to choose ever again."

"Not a choice I will ever make! I promise!"

"I believe that you believe it. But once you are in their hands, I am not sure you will keep believing it."

"Ok, wise man. What is your advice in this situation?"

"My advice? Well M3rqrie. I'll give this advice for free. A personal advice from me to you. And you'll even get my perspective with it. I'm an old man, I've been in this business for as long as I can remember. Before this life, I had another. Wife. Kids. Friends. The path I chose gave me only loneliness, pain, loss. My advice, dear M3rqrie, is simple. Do what we ask of you, bring your loved ones and disappear. Live your life without worry. Help us, and we'll help you. Then you will be truly free. And hopefully happy."

"That is a lot to take in. Not only the advice, but your request as well."

"No worries. I will leave. I have arrangements to make, I'll give you time to digest this. Should you be here when I come back, I'll take it as you will cooperate. If not, then please leave the way you came. And I'll wish you good luck."

With those words he rose from his chair and headed for the corridor to exit, but just before he rounded the corner, he stopped and turned to me again.

"Oh, and don't try to use any of the equipment here. You will not be able to make heads or tails of it. But if your curiosity is too great, by all means try! And a warning. If you leave. You will not be able to enter this facility again."

"How long will you be gone?"

"Don't know, there is food in the kitchen… Sleep on the couch. Bathroom over there."

As he talked he gestured and pointed out the things to me, then left without any other word.

Of course my curiosity was too great, and I immediately sat down in the operator's chair. To my big disappointment he was right. Everything was in Russian, and the control panels were to things I had no idea what they were. I could not even guess.

Passing time

Time moved slowly inside the cage. There was not much to do, after I had walked around and explored every inch of the place, I lay down on the sofa to rest a bit. I fell asleep. I have no idea how long I slept or had been there, but I was still alone in there. No windows, so I could not say if it was day or night. No clock either. The only thing I had to go on was that I was hungry.

I headed for the kitchen and tried to decide what to eat. My options were noodles, noodles or noodles. Only difference was the spices. I hope this was not what he meant with luxury and abundance.

As I ate my thoughts wandered. Choice. What choices did I actually have in this situation? Helping the !y would be like handing over skeleton-keys to the local crime syndicate, after building the bank. Except this was probably on a global scale. Even if half of what he had said was true, it would be very impressive. The worst part was that I believed every word he said. I could not find any plot holes nor any reasons to lie. Except maybe that this was all a lie. But it did not feel like it. It felt real.

This was true agony. Not doing as they requested would be devastating to me, which in all honesty was the current path I was on. Not looking bright on the horizon. The offer would, if it proved valid, set me on a different path in life, and set me up for life. Possibly not alone. The choices were, simplified, do what's right from a moral perspective (not taking into account that I had just done it), and stay hunted, alone and miserable for the rest of my life. Continue to do what I know to be wrong, but gain a life worth living. Heck, at this point I'd settle for the possibility of just living life, without the luxury and abundance. Still it was a hard choice. And Even's advice kept nagging me… if I even considered going along with the request, it would not only affect me, it would also affect her, if I dared dream. And if so, it would not be only my decision. If so, I needed to involve her. Bella.

However you want to measure time, hours, minutes, seconds, they all passed slowly, and I felt like I would go mad inside this horrible cage. I considered leaving more than once, but if there was a remote chance of a future with Bella, I felt like I had to investigate it and check its validity before turning it down.

The return

Then, just like that, life seemed to return and time started its natural course again. The wait was over. I heard the motorized locks of the gate in the far end of the facility. Even returned.

"Good news and bad news! But first I need to know where you stand."

"So much for politeness, straight to the point."

"This is business, we are not friends. I see no point in smalltalk."

"Alright. I am considering your offer. What warranties can you provide that you will keep your word and make me wealthy once I have delivered on my end of the deal?"

"None. Either you do it, and trust us for the duration of your contract, or not. It's up to you."

"And if I need to contact someone to help make my decision."

"Not possible."

"Then my answer will be no, I cannot make this decision alone. I am willing to aid you and do what you ask of me, but if it will be worth anything for me on the other side of the job, I need to know that I will not be alone there. And that is why I need to ask someone something. If it's a no, then I will take my chances and continue alone. If I get a yes, then I'm game. Let's play it!"

"This complicates things."

"That's my answer, and my terms."

"Then I guess the bad news is in your favor. I've secured transport to our destination, that would be the good news. The bad is that we need to wait a few days. Perhaps I could arrange something in that time. Give me a while to figure it out. Who do you need to contact?"

"I won't tell you. Precaution. I just need to make a call."

"No. Out of the question. If this is about to happen, then you need to play by my rules. No phone calls. Where in the world is this person you need to contact?"

"London."

"Well, that is something you've trashed for us. We cannot go there. Not anywhere with cameras. Not anymore. You've put us in a tight position and have complicated every operation significantly. If it were up to me, you should contribute to us as a compensation for the damage you've caused. But I also realize that you acted in good faith, which in reality does not change anything. It is still a mess, and you are still the one who caused it."

Arranging the meet

Even did not speak to me for a long while, instead he sat down in one of the operator's chairs and flicked on various switches, powering up the equipment and started using it. To what end or what he was doing was unclear to me. But after an hour or so, he turned to me again.

"I've arranged for a local courier to deliver a handwritten note to someone somewhere in London. I need to deliver the note in fifteen minutes. There will only be this message. And since you say you need an answer, this message will only communicate a time and a place for a physical meeting. The location and time of the meeting is on this note. I need to get out to deliver the note, you have five minutes to write it."

He handed me a note with a specified time and place and a blank piece of paper, a pen and an envelope.

I was stunned. I could not say how long it had been since I used pen and paper. What could I possibly write to Bella in five minutes? That would make her show up at a specified time and in a place far from London?

The message turned out like this:

"My dear, I am sorry for leaving. It is complicated. I miss you, I want to spend my time with you. I have a question that I need to ask you in person. I hope you can show up and meet me in the docks of Eastbourne now on Sunday at 07.00. I do not know how long we have, things are out of my controle. I love you!"

I put the note in the envelope, sealed it, gave it to Even who was already standing and waiting for it.

"Two things. One. This is very risky, and the risk is yours to take, not mine. You are jeopardizing the both of us, and our transport and all that are affected in this chain of events, including the one that will receive this message. Are you still willing to send it?"

I nodded.

"Second thing then. Who is it for?"

Days in blur

The next few days were a complete blur to me. I had no sense of time, I slept on the sofa when I was tired, I ate noodles when I was hungry. Even on the other hand, seemed to follow a strict protocol and checked each session on his wrist watch, as if to keep track of a schedule that only appeared in his mind. Every now and then he was in one of the operator's seats doing things with all the gizmos and gadgets.

I had no idea if Bella would show up, nor did I have the faintest idea of how to put it to her, nor how much time we would have together. Nor did I know what she would answer. But even so, and I believe it was hope that drove me, I had started to cooperate with Even and had started building and compiling code on an old laptop he provided me with.

Since I knew that it was supposed to run on IoT devices, I wrote some of the subroutines in a low level programming language to get it to run more efficiently and less resource consuming on the devices. This is typically not how you do things these days, but the processors do always operate on this level, so knowing how to write instructions directly to the processors, without the need for one or many translationlayers did indeed speed up the process of having the code executed. The downside would be potential conflicts by sidestepping the established communications protocols, priorities and assigning memory and other in- or output needs of the code. But I figured that if I wrote the basic subroutines, the others could complete it with the specific needs and optimize the interaction with whatever they needed.

Then, our wait seemed over in a flash.

Even started to power up every system there was, plugging in the computer I'd been working on into a communications port of some unknown interface. Then he started something on the computer itself, I could only assume it was some sort of copying protocol to transfer the code to somewhere else, without having to carry the computer around.

Last thing he did, before we headed towards the entrance of the cage, was to open up a safe located behind the kitchen area, and emptied its contents into a black plastic bag. I could not see it all, but it looked like most of it was cash in different currencies.

As we walked out the gate of the cage, Even opened up a little box on the wall revealing a number pad. He entered a twelve digit code and just left the box open.

"Activating the alarm I assume."

"Not really. This place is being shut down. I activated a self destruction sequence with a time delay. As we start the next leg of our little journey, an EMP will set off, leaving every piece of technology in this room utterly useless."

The ride to Bella

When we came out in the open air it was dark. But breathing fresh air again was wonderful! I looked up towards the sky to see if I could see any stars, but it was too cloudy to be able to see any.

"Normally, our protocol states that when traveling two together, we should both know each step of the travelplan. And as often as possible, we should be separated and take different routes. But in this case, I have decided to make exceptions. For many reasons. But the main reason is that we have indications that your little contact stunt may have been compromised. And this is your only warning. Proceed with caution. This is why you will not have any access to information on what happens next. So just tag along and follow me."

With those words he walked away from the house out into the darkness.

Had this been a movie, it would have been a scene where you could do a lot of cool things after, but this is not a movie, and the only thing that actually happened is not very cool at all, I only followed.

We came to a bus stop, uncertain if it was the same that we arrived on, everything looks different in the dark, but I assume as much (even if assume means that I make an ass out of you (u) and me - or as Homer Simpson put it in one of the Simpsons episodes, assumption, makes an ass out of u and mption).

Unlike last time, we boarded the bus together and sat together. Even paid for the tickets with old and worn bills. He noticed that I showed interest in the bills. Luckily he took them from his pocket, where he also returned the change, and not from the black plastic bag. When we sat down he explained to me.

"We only use cash, but not bills from cash machines. We know the tech is available to track bills from cash machines, or withdraws from banks, and since the tech exists, we assume it can be used. And as you probably have figured out, we do not like to be tracked." He nodded towards the black bag.

I heard what he said, but I wasn't focused. My mind was fully occupied with wondering whether Bella would show up or not. And what I would tell her, and how. Million thoughts.

On our way to the destination we changed buses a few times, and as the sun started to rise over the horizon, we got off a bus at the Eastbourne marina.

The question

My feet hadn't even landed on the ground before my eyes started to search for Bella.

Even laid a hand on my shoulder.

"We are early. It's only 6 o'clock."

It was a terrible wait. We sat on a bench near a closed Ice cream bar. Luckily there was a clock on the wall, so I could follow the hands on the watch face as they slowly dragged themselves around their predetermined course.

We did not say anything. Just sat there waiting.

About a quarter to seven a car pulled up, and someone got out. Bella. My lovely Bella!

I ran to her. She looked puzzled, even a little hurt. And perhaps a bit angry as well, but when we held each other it was as if time itself dissolved and I could just breathe her in, feeling her warmth. I have no idea how long we stood there, but apparently time did not move slow anymore. She was the first to talk.

"What is all this about?"

"First, I am sorry. I never meant things to be like this. But I am in a tricky situation."

"Because of *them*?"

"Yes. And another player in the same scene."

"Another, how many are there?"

"Apparently more than I could anticipate, and more than I know. I don't know how much time I have. There is something I need to ask you."

"I really hope you are asking me to marry you, because there is no other question I would have driven all the way here, this early in the morning to get to answer."

I knew she was partly joking, to relieve tension, but at the same time, I understood the seriousness in it.

"What if I would ask you to marry me, what would you say?"

"Yes, of course..."

"Even if it meant that you had to leave everything you know behind, possibly without saying goodbye, and then live somewhere else with me..."

She looked at me...

"Don't know, ask me and you'll see..."

"Alright..." I took her head between my hands, looked her deeply in the eyes, kissed her gently and then took a deep breath:

"Will you marry me?"

Departure

As soon as I had asked the question, Even yelled at me that it was time to go.

I looked at Bella, waiting for an answer…

"Yes, but you need to redo this proposal… But yes, I will marry you and go with you wherever you need to go!"

I got tears in my eyes and kissed her again.

"Now!" Even yelled louder.

"I'll find a way to contact you, my love! Thank you for showing up!"

And with those words I left her there at the dock and headed back to Even who had climbed down in a small boat. There was a man driving the boat and the motor was still running. I had not heard it approach, probably was too busy with focusing on Bella.

As soon as I was safely on board, the boat backed out from the harbor and out into the open water. My eyes were fixed on Bella, as she still stood where I had left her. She did not wave. I did not wave. We only looked at eachother. Another movie moment that did not turn out as it would have in a movie. I felt tears dripping. Mixed joy and happiness with sadness and loneliness. I needed to sort this mess. And now I was highly motivated to do so.

Also… I would soon have a wife… surreal as ever…

When I could no longer see the marina on the sureline, I turned my eyes away from the spot where I imagined Bella still was standing watching after me, I turned to Even. He had not said anything for the entire time, and I was grateful for it. But now he talked.

"Remember, the risk was yours to take. I will not be held responsible for whatever happens next. Our journey, however, has just begun. Now it's safe to tell you the traveling plans. We will shortly arrive at another boat, it is a fishing boat, we will take it to France. There we will use local buses and trains to get to the other side of France, to the mediterranean. There, a chain of boats will take us to Istanbul. In Istanbul we'll meet up with the others. I assume you still want to honor our deal?"

"I do." but in my head, I said it to Bella at our wedding, more than to Even on the boat.

After a while of silence I had to ask:

"Why all these complicated traveling arrangements? Would it not be easier to just take a flight directly to Istanbul, or a regular train?"

"Easier, yes, for them to catch us. For them to find out where we are and where we are going. Thanks to you they have the ability to do so. Are they using that ability to track us? Maybe. But like I said before. If the tech is there to use, we assume it is being used. So, all travels are limited to unregistered tickets, paid by cash on local trains and buses. And fishermen who are friends with unregistered money. Let's just say that we do not ask for a receipt."

The long trip

I got to tell you, I am not cut out for a trip of that magnitude. Even however, seemed to be unaffected. As if he had all the time in the world. Being present on each seat on each bus and each train, as if that seat was the entire world at the time.

Me on the other hand, I just wanted to get to Istanbul to complete the job, get the money, and then leave all this behind me. It felt like each new seat was another obstacle to get passed. Again, time seemed to shift into different gears, and everything seemed super slow. ("Patience, young Padawan." as some quote Star Wars. But it is debated if there even was someone who uttered those exact words. I'll need to resee the movies and the series again to be able to be sure, but I believe it is Anakin who said them to Ashoka, and not Yoda who said them to Luke, as often claimed. Who said it or if it was ever said at all, at this point my patience was zero!)

In hindsight, it was probably a good thing that we spent all that time traveling, changing seats, means of transportation, on water, on land, on water, again on land. From Evens perspective, we managed to move from London, through France, crossing several borders and ending up in Istanbul without ever showing our passport, getting caught on any camera or registered in any ticket systems. From my perspective I got a lot of time to sort my thoughts. Most of them were fixed on Bella, our wedding, how I wanted to propose to her in a proper way, and how and where we should spend our lives together. Some circulated the more sensitive subject of what she gave up to be with me, and if I was worth her sacrifice, and how I possibly ever could compensate for that sacrifice.

Other parts of me focused on the technical solutions up ahead. I knew that this would be more challenging than the things I did for the N3v3r!and, given the infrastructure I had to get the code to operate within. No matter if it was native within the IoT devices, which I assumed would be the logical place to put it, or if it was in the dynamic virtual infrastructure on the resource pool from the IoT-devices, there was a vast number of various challenges to be dealt with. A part of me actually enjoyed the situation and looked forward to the upcoming work.

How we managed to get all the way to Istanbul I do not know, but like that, we arrived, last part of the way in a local Dolmus. I have never been as afraid of riding in any vehicle as I was that part of the trip. The driver was insane! That ride marked the end of the infinitely long journey, and the start of the next chapter in this story.

Even guided to another door, this time it was inside a club, again another movie scene, even a cliché movie scene. A door in the back of the club, this also with their symbol, hand painted, but not with a brush this time. It looked more like it had been sprayed on, !y in red.

Before we entered, Even turned to me, and spoke close to my ear to penetrate the loud music that still surrounded us.

"I know I have already told you about Reacher, and I understand that you don't like him before you've even met him. I respect that. But I want to apologize in advance. I have no idea what he will say to you, but I am sure that he will piss you off more than once and in more than one way. But I also want to remind you that you have chosen to collaborate with us, and that you will be well compensated once you've done what we ask of you."

And with those words, he turned towards the door and opened it, not giving me any time or opportunity to reply.

Part II

The job

Meeting the !y

Behind the door in the club in Istanbul was a familiar sight. The same basic principle as I had seen in England. Except that this cage seemed larger, more equipped and a lot newer than the other I had visited.

As if he could read my thoughts, Even turned to me and said:

"We've built all this for this purpose only. Once you are done, we will initiate the self-destruct here as well and our paths will part ways. We will go our way, and you, well, that is entirely up to you."

"Isn't it a waste of resources? Building this and then having it self-destruct?"

"We take our privacy very seriously. Nothing is a waste when it comes to protecting it. Now, let's meet the others."

The first one we ran into was Virtual. He did not say much, only nodded in my general direction, keeping his eyes on the monitor, deeply into what he was doing. Then came Reacher, or, as I learned pretty quickly, Preacher. That was his current state of mind.

"Welcome princess!" He exclaimed as soon as he saw me!

"Nice to meet you! It's rare to have a girl visiting us."

He needed less than two words to start getting on my nerves, and by the thirteenth he pissed me off, big time.

"I assume you know I am non-binary?"

"I know you think you are, but sorry princess, God only created two kinds of people. Boys and girls. You were born either one or the other, regardless of how you feel. And in your case. Girl."

In less than thirty seconds he had managed to push more trigger points than most people I knew, except maybe for my brother. But this one even out performed my brother on the annoyance-scale. By light years.

Even signed to Preacher to be quiet, and I figured it was not time to start an argument, besides, I felt like I needed to be the bigger person of the two of us and try to keep the relationship professional at all times, no matter how annoying he became. It was only this job and then I would never have to see him again.

The first part of the job

I will not move too much in advance, and I will come to the point soon, but the time spent in Istanbul was divided in two parts for me. A before and after. Marked by a conversation I had with Even where he shared painful information with me. I will come to it shortly. What is common for both the before and the after is that again, time seemed to be in a different gear.

The first part was intense work with implementing and adapting the code, working closely with both Virtual and Reacher. In retrospect I believe I was the one who learned the most, and got the most out of the deal, and I almost forgot it was a job to be done. I enjoyed the process.

Seeing what the asshole and Virtual had built, each on his own, was super impressive. I even learned that Virtual had created a parallel infrastructure to provide resources for his dynamic virtual platform. He had written various programs and apps that were widely spread and used, and with the consent of the user in the EULA (End-user License Agreement) that the program or app was free to use, but that they approved a small usage (less than 0,1%) of their local resources to be used by the developers for various usages, among others for diagnostic and behavioral analysis. Now, it is widely known that no one reads the EULA's, but they are legally binding nevertheless. Like public Wifi, there have been experiments with putting things like "I promise to give up my first born in order to use this Wifi-connection." And people do not read, only want the Wifi-connection and click the "Agree-button" without reading. (Which is also brilliant for hackers, who have set up 'free' access points where there are a lot of people, gaining access to a lot of information.)

Sorry, I'm rambling a bit, trying to avoid the painful event that is coming soon.

I did not get to leave the facility for the duration of the work, in fact, the only one who left occasionally was Even. And again, I lost track of time completely, not knowing if it was day or night. And the constant music that flooded through the walls did not contribute to anything else than disconnecting me further from the world outside.

In there the only thing that existed was the code, the systems and delivering the work. Then, all of a sudden, when the work was almost done, Even requested a private talk with me, and took me aside.

The second part of the job

It changed everything for me. Even told me that Bella had been kidnapped by the N3v3r!and and was held hostage somewhere, exactly where, he was unsure, but promised to find out if I wanted him to.

Of course I wanted him to!

When he told me it was like a bitchslap in the face, while someone took a big heavy punch against my stomach.

But it also lit a new fire within me, putting fuel on an already intense fire.

I intensified my efforts and got the work done, and when it was done, oh, what a fine work we'd performed. It worked smooth and seamless, as a well integrated part of the core functions in each platform.

This part of the job was conflicting when it comes to time. On one hand, it was painfully slow, agony, all I wanted was to get the job done, to be able to focus on meeting the N3v3r!and and getting my Bella back, and on the other hand, time seemed to rush by in an instant.

By that time, I almost felt like a part of the !y. But it all came to an abrupt end as the job was done.

Even followed me out of the door we entered and I was back in the world, in a club. I had not said goodbye to the others, and for a moment I thought Even would leave me there and go back inside. But luckily he didn't.

As we got out of the club he turned to me.

"You have held up your end of the deal, I will hold up my end. Here is an address and a name, just say I sent you, and he'll know what to do."

He handed me a piece of paper, with something scribbled on it.

"I will give you two more things. Temporary access to the platform you've just helped us improve, to do what you please. You can find your friend, you can erase yourself from the face of the earth for all I care. It is up to you, I'll give you one month, then you will be locked out. The other thing I want to provide you with is a location. It will be given to you by the man on the note."

He turned around without saying anything else and went back inside. That was the last I ever saw of Even, or the other two for that matter.

The Broker

There I found myself, on a sidewalk somewhere in Istanbul, without phone and computer, only a note with a name and address. Luckily I still had a lot of money in my bag, but I figured that pound was not the best currency to use in Turkey.

At the time I did not reflect on just how exposed I was in that moment, but it occured to me later on. Should anything have happened to me then and there, nobody would ever find out or care. But nothing happened, except that I figured out my next move. I needed somewhere to go to set up a temporary base and plan my next move. The second obviously being finding the person on the note, so what would my first move be?

The choice fell at a nearby hotel. They looked strangely at me when I wanted to pay cash with pound bills rather than with a credit card. But I got a room for the night and paid for a decent meal. !y are great at many things, but hospitality and food is not their forté.

Even if my thoughts constantly circulated to Bella, I felt exhausted, but pushed myself to continue. After my dinner, I took a long shower and lay down on the soft bed and probably dozed off immediately. I was woken up by the sunlight that came through the window.

After a big breakfast, I ordered a taxi (no more dolmos for me) and prepaid it in the hotel lobby. I did not know what to expect when I arrived, but whatever I could imagine, it would not have been close to where I got.

As the taxi pulled up at the address, I saw a red and white flag, and the house was one of many with different flags waving outside. I wasn't sure, but I believed I had just been taken to an embassy area, and sure enough, I was at the Moroccan embassy, and obviously I was expected. As soon as I mentioned the name on my note, their hospitality increased significantly.

I was taken to a room and was brought a wide selection of drinks, spanning from tea and coffee to whisky, wine and champagne. But I decided to wait for my host before indulging in any drinks. Besides, I was still full from the fabulous breakfast at the hotel.

I did not have to wait long before a man entered the room and closed the doors behind him. He felt like a servant, yet with respectful confidence.

"May I offer you a drink?" he said, looking directly at me.

"Will you drink with me?"

"Yes. If you wish."

"Then I will have whatever you are having."

He then turned his attention to the cart where everything stood ready to be served and made two cups of tea. Not what I expected, but in a way I was relieved.

"This is Kusmi tea, the French tradition of direct descendants from the tea maker of the Russian Tsar. They fled to Paris in the revolution, taking their knowledge with them and started a very lucrative business. The flavor of the day is Kashmir Tchai."

He handed me a cup and took his own and offered me a chair by a table and took a seat for himself.

"Before we begin our business, I need to ask, who sent you?"

"Even."

"I suspected so, he said you would be coming soon."

"The name of the card is a front name, and this is not a real embassy. It is also a front. You will know me as the broker, and I am assigned to you today to make the arrangements that you were promised by Even."

The arrangements

"I am not entirely sure exactly what he promised me, except that I would be very wealthy."

"Well, M3rqrie, I am afraid that 'very wealthy' would be an understatement."

"How so?"

"Let's just say, for the sake of argument, that money will be the least of your problems after today."

"That sounds about right, but, if I may ask, what would my problems be?"

"Ah, like always, everything is perspective and choice."

"So, what you are saying is that I choose my own problems."

"No, I say that you will need to choose the solution to your problems. Then face the consequences."

I let his words sink in, as I sipped on the tea. It was truly marvelous.

"Alright, how do we do this?"

"First, I'll need to take your fingerprints and retinal scan. Then I will connect them to various accounts, spread world wide, untraceable."

"How much money are we talking about?"

"Hard to say, it keeps increasing, since there are continuously being transfers made to the accounts. But if you would like to buy a small country, I believe you would be able to."

"And how do I access these accounts?"

"That is up to you. The accounts are not registered to any name, only to your biometric prints that I take here today. You need only to visit any Broker office anywhere in the world, then we will arrange access to whatever you need."

"Whatever I need?"

"Yes. Whatever you need."

"Well, today I need a few things. I'd like to go to wherever Even informed you about, but I do not have any passport or traveling documents. And I would like to have two computers with certain specifications, a phone, satellite connections and a place where I could work from for an unspecified period. But let's say a month to start with. And if you don't mind, where am I going?"

"It shall be done. And London is the place Even specified. Now, if *you* don't mind, would you like me to get the readings and complete that part of today's business?"

He pulled up a device with something that looked like a biometric scanner for handprints and with a retinal scanner. After scanning my eyes and my hands, he excused himself and exited. When he came back a moment later, he had a computer and a phone with him.

"Now, this phone is your best friend from now on. Have it on you always. And yes, before you ask, we can track you and your whereabouts, but no one else can. Courtesy of the !y.
All our clients have one of these, and it lets us send you information, and it lets you send us your requests. The phone is programmed to your access only, and it is encrypted with far better things than I can explain to you, but I am sure you will figure it out as soon as you start using it."

He handed me the phone.

"As for the specifications of the equipment, please write them down here."

He handed me the computer with an open document. Took me a few minutes to specify everything I wanted.

"Now, should there be anything else, just open the phone and I'm sure you will figure out how to contact us. We have a plane ready for you in about two hours, and a limousine will take you to the airport. Would it be anything else at this time?"

"Yes, one more thing."

The broker listened carefully.

The new operating center

I was booked on a private jet back to London, and waiting for me as I got off the plane was an unmarked car with a driver. The driver's instructions were to take me to my temporary place of work, but via the billboards of Piccadilly Circus.

When we passed the billboards, I smiled and felt pretty good about myself. They were covered with my ad, as I had specified to the Broker.

"N3v3r!and, I'm coming for you", and with Uncle Sam pointing at each and every person passing. Sure enough, most people would not understand it at all, but I suspected that word would spread to those who would understand it. And my goal was to show them that I was not afraid of them.

I could get used to this, private drivers, people obeying my wishes and performing what I asked them to do. But it wasn't me… I would not be comfortable living my life like that. But I enjoyed the opportunity to try.

My driver stopped in front of a big house, and he handed me the keys to the front door. Then he took off.

As I entered I was unsure of what my next steps would be, but as always, it had to start with gathering information. First I needed to verify the intel I had gotten from Even.

The tech I had specified was located in a big room that I believe was meant for having big dinner parties. But now there were only my things on the ridiculously big table.

Before I even checked the rest of the house, I assembled everything I needed and started to equip the computers with what I needed.

One of the computers was for public use, the one I would use to access the internet and the darknet and use to communicate with the N3v3r!and. The other was connected to Virtual's platform with the new tools for camera access, facial recognition and the sweeper tool available at my fingertips. For a month.

I gave myself three weeks, tops. Then I should have freed Bella. And proposed. At least freed her.

Confirming

My first mission was to confirm the intel Even had provided. That they had taken my Bella and kept her somewhere against her will.

Somehow I could not believe that the N3v3r!and would be capable of doing something like that, but I had also learned not to underestimate them.

Sadly, it turned out to be true. Took me a little over a week to track her from the last point of contact. They had kidnapped her after work and held her captive at some kind warehouse in the outskirts of London, south west. Fortunately for me, the security system they used to keep her under surveillance was a system that was available through Reachers' brilliant work. (Yes, he is still an asshole, but a brilliant asshole!)

Once I knew the location, I researched the surroundings and checked the facility to evaluate my options. Again, I felt like James Bond or some super secret agent, and again, this would be a really cool movie scene.

I tried to communicate with Bella, but the equipment had only the option to listen to what was going on there, not send any audio in return. To my big relief, she was unharmed. I found out that there was a small LED on the camera unit, and I got it to flash, in red, at least I think I did. But she did not see it. Without knowing if she would be able to understand it, I programmed the LED to send the text "will you marry me" in morse code. And I looped it, hoping she would see it, and perhaps understand that there was a pattern to it, and hopefully understand it was me, even if she would not get the message.

I switched computers and from the other I used about 25 jumpstations and relays to send a message to N3v3r!and. Using my own real account. After all, I had already notified them that I was on to them.

"What are your terms?"

I got a reply within a minute.

"Return to us and rejoin, then she will be released."

"Is that all?"

"Let's discuss!"

"When and where?"

"How about now? At the office?"

"No way! Not safe for me to come to the belly of the beast! I choose time and location. I'll get in touch!!"

Then I terminated the communications link, scrambled my tracks (a little like blowing on a house of cards, except that I did not just blow on them, I launched a tornado against them).

Something did not feel right.

Communication

I tried to figure out a plan on how to rescue the love of my life. But let's face it, I am no James Bond. I am a hacker. I am good at hacking, at digging up information, snooping around in other people's secrets, compromising systems, and gaining access. Information is my game. Not field operations, and definitely not rescue operations.

I played around with different scenarios. I could use resources through the Broker. I could... Yes, what could I do... Oh, my love... perhaps it would be best to just surrender.

And just then, I noticed something when I checked the videofeed from Bella. She had, using I do not know what, created a pattern on the wall.

- .-- . ...

That was morse code. - . - - is Y, . is E and ... is S. Yes!

My Bella knew morse code! She said yes! She had seen my message and she said yes!

It worked! I reprogrammed the message. I L U, or I Love You. Just to let her know I had seen it.

And a little later on, I got a reply: ..- ..---

. . - is U . . - - - is 2.

A way of communication! Lovely. Slow, but it was there.

This gave me hope.

I could send her information.

And information was, and has always been my greatest tool.

This was my advantage in this situation. Information. And, perhaps, just a little manipulation of the information. Hacker style.

A plan started to form.

The first thing I did was to shut down the LED on the camera. In case the intrusion would get noticed, and to let Bella know what to do when it was time. I hoped she would understand that turning down the message was only to prepare to send another. I just needed to figure out what.

The rescue plan

First thing first. As they say. The personnel at the warehouse were employees. They were scheduled. Their schedule was digital, and communication regarding the schedule was digital. Digital information, hmm... who do I know that would be able to manipulate that. Well, oh, yeah, that's right, that would be me! Suck it James Bond, this is something you would not be able to do!

A quick search on the internet gave me a big window of opportunity. As a hacker, I am not into sports, but the guards at the warehouse might be. I hoped anyway, which is why a London football derby between Chelsea and Tottenham seemed like a good opportunity. A change in their work schedules giving the scheduled guards the night off, except for one, I could not leave the place completely empty. No one would buy that.

The derby provided me with another thing. A crowded place to meet. Or at least, set up a meeting that would seem legit.

I used the Broker to get a car waiting outside the warehouse. One passenger only. Waiting outside the north-east door, engine hot. I specified a red car, not because it was ideal, but red was the color with the least amount of letters. The message I programmed to Bella was:

Signal left left right left red car.

My plan was simple. I would set off the fire alarm - the signal. At the same time I would open up all the electronic locks in the entire building. As Bella got out of the room she was locked in, she would turn left, then left at the first corridor, then right and left again to get to the door that led out to where the red car would wait to pick her up.

At the same time the N3v3r!and would be engaged in a meeting that would take place at the game. They would probably direct all their attention there. To be able to catch me as well, if that was their intention. I mean, if they held Bella, who had nothing to do with this, except that she is important to me, then I imagined that they would be able to do things to me as well.

I programmed the LED of the camera again and I used the other computer, again with jumps all over the world, and I sent the time and place to the N3v3r!and. I did not mention that there would be a game at that time, or at that place, I figured that it would be a possibility that they would not be aware of it, which only would add to my advantage. I specified a time and a place, a section of the arena in about the same time where it would be game pause, and near a place where they, at least according to the information I could find online, sold both beer and hot dogs. I mean, London football derby, beer and hot dogs, what could possibly generate more crowds in England? I could not imagine anything.

The game was two days away. Two long days.

It all seemed simple enough. The hard part was to wait.

Executing

I made a few last minute changes. The red car, I redirected it to a private airport instead of to the house. I ordered a car from the house to the same airport. I arranged for a private plane to take us to Madrid. And several other private planes that would travel empty to various other destinations from the same airport at the same time.

And then I transferred all available funds from the accounts the Broker had provided me with, and all the funds I had in my old accounts to new untraceable accounts in a few different banks world wide. The numbers were breathtaking.

In Madrid, I arranged for a safe house for a few days, giving us time to talk things through and plan our next steps together.

The wait was long. And I followed the movements of the guards at the warehouse, I followed the N3v3r!and people. I tracked the crowd in the arena. I checked the red car and everything seemed to work out as planned.

As the game started, there was only one remaining guard at the warehouse, and he was busy watching the game. I could not have asked for a better opportunity. As the game was about to get close to the paus, and the guard had taken some well needed steps towards the toilet, giving him enough time to start, I remotely triggered the fire alarm, and opened up all the doors in Bellas path to the red car.

Sure enough, as the alarm started, the guard on duty panicked in the toilet and hurried to the best of his ability and rushed back to check his monitors to see if he could see any fire, giving me time to lock the doors between him and Bella. And shutting him inside the operations office.

As I started the alarm, there was full activity at the N3v3r!and people in the arena, and I assumed they guessed that I would not show up.

On pure instinct, I had not planned it, I activated the sweeping protocol on me, and got a confirmation that the job started. But when I started it for Bella, I got access denied. And at the same time I was thrown out of the other !y systems as well. Despite the month I got promised by Even, I was cut short.

Now I had lost eyes on the ground, and could only hope that what I had set in motion would stay in motion and work out. I left everything as it was and exited to the waiting car and it was a long nervous ride to the airport.

To Madrid

My car was the first to arrive, since I was a lot closer to the air-field.

I had no way of contacting the driver of the red car. I could probably arrange it, I only brought two things from the house, my bag with clothes and cash and the Broker phone. But I figured I had started the chain reaction, and I did not want to jeopardize anything that would risk stopping or slowing down the events.

I can not describe the joy when the red car arrived. I won't even try. But at that moment, it felt like the most important moment of my entire life. Everything had led up to this very moment.

It was a happy reunion, and hectic, we ran to the plane that was just about to take off.

I felt like a child on the airplane, reunited with my best friend in the entire world, and we were about to run away on our very own adventure!

We had a lot of catching up to do on the plane, and I explained the entire situation with what I had done at the N3v3r!and, what I found out about them, how the !y had helped me and how I needed to help them in order and what I got out of it.

Bella told me about her misery as I left, and how she got a message from me asking her to meet up, but it turned out not to be from me, and that is when she was taken. It made me so angry that they would go so low that they used her to get to me.

Then I remembered, I was so curious.

"I did not know you knew morse code!"

"I didn't when I met you, but I've learned."

"Why?"

"Remember the Art Books books I gave you?"

"Yes!"

"Well, on one of the pages there was morse-code, and I wanted to decipher it, and my academic history-buff-brain kind of absorbed it."

"Wow! I'm impressed!"

"Well, you know morse as well, so why is it impressive?"

"I don't, I know about morse, and I can look it up and use it, but I do not know it!"

We laughed at it, and I silently thanked this Art Books for making my Bella curious about morse-code. I have no idea what would have happened if she hadn't learned it.

Arriving in Madrid

We landed and had a car waiting, as per ordered from the Broker. It took us directly to the safe house, and our first priority was to grab something to eat.

Being responsible for making traveling arrangements, I still had a lot to learn, like planning food. Bella was starving, not literally, but her previous 'hotel' did not exactly serve the best food. Let's say that their chef was not exactly 5 star quality, not even 1 star quality, more like, uhm, fresh graduate from microwave restaurant school. With low grades. Barely passed the exams.

We found a local tavern just around the corner from our rented apartment, and we stayed there until it was closing time, and we had spent the past hours under blankets in the star-spangled cold night, enjoying various desserts and hot drinks. I'll always remember their hot chocolate with cinnamon.

It was well beyond midnight when we returned to our temporary home.

Both tired from everything that had happened recently, and exhausted from our marathon talk at dinner, we fell asleep in eachothers arms and I do not think that I moved an inch the entire night. It feels like I woke up exactly where I fell asleep, still in the arms of my lovely Bella, and she still in mine.

That morning we had breakfast on our balcony in the early Spanish morning sun, with a view over the surrounding rooftops, listening to the city slowly waking up. A truly magical morning.

We had talked and talked for hours on end the day before, and still had a million things to talk about, but that morning, in the sun, with a hot steaming cup of tea each, we enjoyed the silence and eachothers company. I held Bellas hand and every now and then I could not resist an impulse to snuggle it or kiss it.

Before lunch we went on a shopping tour, to buy food and clothes for us both. Since we had not decided where to go next, we kept the shopping to basic needs only. And keeping luggage light.

More?

That afternoon we spent on our balcony, in the shadows, resting, talking.

Then Bella asked a critical question.

"First N3v3r!and and the shadow people, then the !y. Are there any more of them that we need to worry about?"

"To be honest, I don't know. But I doubt it. I mean, the N3v3r!and is a big mystery online. A legend that is hard to grasp, even for me, and I've spent a lot of time searching. They operate on the darknet, and on the internet, but hidden. They protect, cooperate and are protected by powerful people in the shadows. Then, as Even expressed it, in the sewers, there are the !y, balancing the N3v3r!and. Every action creates a reaction. Like in physics."

"But what if there is someone hiding in the ocean? Like Nemo. Or in the sky like Shield? Or hiding in plain sight?"

"...or on the dark side of the moon?"

"Or on the dark side of the moon..."

We were silent a while, both in our own thoughts. I was the first to speak.

"It would be cool if there was someone on the moon, I'd like to go there if I could. But I find it highly unlikely that there could exist any more powerful organizations, seems to me like the world is already divided, and the pieces taken. I mean, what else can there be to fight over? Crimelords have the underground, with drugs and weapons. The population is in check and are asleep, pawns in a big chess game. The only thing I could see possible is if someone shares my ideas about liberating people from the system, but I already feel that the !y have taken that position, even if they have chosen a different arena and a different approach. Then again, what do I know? I have been wrong before!"

"Well, you are still wonderful, even if you are wrong!"

"Babe, what have I done to be so lucky to have you?"

"You put your nose in business that you had no part in, and if you hadn't, we wouldn't have met, so I am glad you are curious!"

We were interrupted by a sound from the Broker phone that I had left inside.

The message

"We regret to inform you that your traveling companion has an arrest warrant issued by Interpol, for aiding an infamous digital terrorist. This complicates our arrangements further. We will still do our best to meet your requirements."

"Sounds like the N3v3r!and has brought their game to the next level. I assume I am the digital terrorist you are aiding, and that there is no arrest warrant for me, since I do not exist in the system anymore. Now you are a fugitive and on the run from justice."

I looked at Bella, but she only continued to smile and did not seem worried at all.

"Well, at least I have a handsome and sexy digital terrorist, that I am pleased to aid in whatever way I can! Besides, I have never been in trouble with the law before. Not even a speeding ticket or wrong parking. Nothing. Feels kind of exciting to be in trouble."

I could not help but to admire her. Brave soul! But this complicated things further.

"If you are wanted by the Interpol, you will most likely be identified as soon as we set foot in an airport or if we try to go through customs somewhere. And they will be notified."

"I know that look on your face. You have a plan, don't you?"

"Well, at least part of a plan, let's work it out together."

My plan was incomplete, but I had an old client in Egypt, who specialized in getting false papers and documents, even passports. If we could go there, inspired by the !y method of traveling, we could probably get what we would need to be able to travel anywhere legit. But we needed to go somewhere where we could disappear in plain sight. Perhaps to America. And I also had the nagging feeling that we should ditch the Brooker and make our way without them. It was not a feeling I could explain or give any reasons to, just a shadow of a doubt in my mind. Gut feeling. (And not gut as in the German word for good.)

We talked it over for a while, and then we had a plan. But we needed the rest of the day to prepare a few things, so we took another shopping tour in the city, and stayed out late and had a fabulous dinner at Restaurante Sacha, perfect for a two person date with candles and a true romantic feeling. Another movie moment. We made sure to stay on crowded streets together, and in places where there were likely to be cameras. With our faces well visible at all times, no shades, no caps, no fancy hair do.

Leaving Madrid

The next day, we got up early and enjoyed breakfast outdoors in the sunrise. Early breakfast to go in a big city like Madrid is served about the same time the clubs close.

Then we used the Broker phone to make arrangements to leave Madrid.

The instructions were like this:

- A car from our safehouse to the private airport.
- Three private planes with different destinations.
  - One bound for Oslo in Norway. There, a waiting car to take us wherever we requested.
  - One bound for Budapest in Hungary. There, a waiting car to take us wherever we requested.
  - One bound for Athens in Greece. There, a waiting car to take us wherever we requested.
- At the airport in Madrid, three different private rooms where we could talk to the staff for instructions before takeoff - obviously we would only be on one of the planes, so we needed to meet the staff of each plane in private to ensure our instructions would be followed.
- All three of the planes should report their destinations according to above instructions, but they should be aware that a change of destination might occur mid air.

All scheduled and executed as quickly as possible, and we awaited confirmation and a car to arrive at our location. We packed our things in newly bought backpacks.

Soon, the car arrived, and it took us directly to the private airport and we were taken to the private rooms where staff from each plane was waiting. All three knew of each other, and all three knew that there was a one in three chance that they might get passengers, and a two in three chance that they would fly an empty plane.

In the first room, where the staff heading for Oslo were, our instructions were like this. A package for delivery at an address in Helsinki. About 30 minutes after take off, they should request a course change and reroute to Helsinki in Finland instead, and when they had landed, make sure the package got delivered as fast as possible. They understood they would not carry any passengers and left the room after they had gotten their instructions.

In the second room, where the staff heading for Budapest were, our instructions were like this. A package for delivery at an address in Prague. About 30 minutes after take off, they should request a course change and reroute to Prague in Czech Republic instead. And when they had landed, make sure the package got delivered as fast as possible. They understood that they would not carry any passengers and left the room after they had gotten their instructions.

In the third room, where the staff heading for Athens were, our instructions were like this. A package for delivery at an address in Istanbul. About 30 minutes after take off, they should request a course change and reroute to Istanbul in Turkey instead. And when they had landed, make sure the package got delivered as fast as possible. They understood that they would not carry any passengers and left the room after they had gotten their instructions.

We waited a while at the airport, then took our backpacks and walked out of there.

The addresses in the various cities we had checked using the Broker phone. All packages had some kind of content. but the package going to Istanbul contained the Broker phone. Thought it would be best to return it to where it came from, even if it was an address at random, and not actually where it came from.

Should someone try to track us, they could confirm our presence in Madrid yesterday. They could confirm us arriving at the airport, they could confirm that my phone was traveling to Istanbul and being delivered to an address there. But with a little luck, they could not confirm that we walked out of the airport, took a bus out of Madrid, found our way down through Spain to Gibraltar, and by boat to Morocco, and then local buses and trains to Egypt. At least that was what we hoped. To make luck swing our way, we did what we could to help, by changing clothes and taking on sunglasses and caps before leaving the airport. This was like another movie moment, an actual movie moment. Bella quickly coloured her hair black before we left.

Part III

Leaving

Escape

Now, for someone like me, it is very hard to resist the temptation of using digital aids when having a task to perform. But for this part of the journey, and this part of the plan, it was essential not to leave any traces behind. And how do you find someone that does not want to be found, and that is not expecting you, without revealing that you are there and looking for that person? To complicate things even further, we've never actually met in real life, only online.

But if you remember, hacking is not only about technical skills, it is also about social skills and knowing how to get what you want out of people without them knowing what you are after.

Took me a while to ask around in general requests not to raise questions, but after a while, I had a pretty good idea of where to look, what to ask and who to ask.

Deciding to play it as safe as possible, Bella and I got dressed for a nice dinner, booked us a table for two, and asked the waiter to take a note to the bar, with instructions that the bartender would know what to do with the note.

It said: *"Echo Sierra Charlie. Tower is moving. Need cover. 4D as in Muddhedd."*

My hope was that the bartender would be clever enough to decode the first part, Echo Sierra Charlie. ESC. Escape. Which was the covername of my former client. He said it was for helping people to escape. The rest would be indecipherable for the bartender and only meant for ESC's eyes. Tower is moving, meaning that I was on the move. When we communicated through the channels of the dark web, and he wanted my help, he often used chess terms, and my designation was the tower. Need cover, was just to communicate that I needed help, and just the kind of help he was offering to his clients. 4 D is the hexadecimal code for M, short for M3rqrie, and there just happens to be 4 d's in Muddhedd (who also starts with an M), an artist we discussed on occasion, which I added to underline that it was me that wanted to contact him.

We enjoyed our dinner, with a nice appetizer Hawawshi, a sort of stuffed bread, followed by a main course Koshari, something that felt like a mishmash of various ingredients, but oh, so tasteful! And by the time we got to the desert, we'd just ordered Baklava and Koshari, the first being some kind of cake and the latter a kind of tea, when a man approached our table.

The dance

"Being a gentleman, I would offer one of you to dance. And my prejudice tells me that my dancing partner for this dance would be a redhead. But now I am talking from my prejudice only, and I could be wrong! If so, my apologies!"

"I am more protective of my queen than I would be of any king in the game. Why would you not dance with me?"

"To be honest, I am not sure how to dance with a tower, who would lead? I am not sure I would be comfortable in following someone else's lead in the dance."

"Then perhaps there will be no dance at all. Maybe this whole conversation would just be a big misunderstanding?" I looked at the man, who clearly knew who I was, but who I still wasn't sure was the man we were looking for. So I decided to test him.

"Let's say that we need *Escape*. Which theme song would be the best choice?"

"For You (*4 U*), depends if you are in *the beginning* or if this is your *last voyage*?"

He certainly knew his Muddhedd songs, and could very well be the man we were looking for.

"And if we need more than tickets to get where we need to go? What would your advice be?"

"My advice then, based on whispers in the dark, is that like Ikaros, you are flying too close to the sun. Perhaps my papers can provide a little shade, but they would not protect you from the heat. But providing shade from the sun is not as profitable as letting the sun's heat get to you. Then again, papers may get an old friend out of trouble, so that alone would be worth the effort."

Ah, the word was out on the dark web, I was missing, and it sounded as if there was a reward out from the N3v3r!and. Even so, we would get the help we needed. I wondered how much Bella understood by this cryptic talk, but I assumed she got the most of it.

"Then I would suggest we do dance, but perhaps not here. If you'll lead, we will follow."

Getting papers

Even if we had not gotten our dessert yet, we followed the man who led us out from the restaurant and showed us into a waiting car.

"I am sorry to cut your dinner short, but I am in the middle of a lot of things. I hope you don't mind the interruption."

"Apology accepted, and thank you for coming to our aid. As you've probably understood, we are in the middle of something that is a bit over our heads."

"I imagine so, but I must say, I did not expect you to show up at my doorstep. But I am pleased that you did. I will do whatever I can to meet your needs. Now, I will take you to my studio, where we will do a photoshoot, and you will need to specify what kind of papers you want, then I will get to work on them. But as I said earlier, I am in the middle of a lot of things, so I can not be the host I'd like to be. But I can offer you a safe haven for the duration of my work."

We arrived at what he called his studio, which was a small room in a basement, where he advertised with terrible pictures of couples getting married. Anyone who passed the studio window would keep walking, even if they were looking for a photographer to take pictures. I knew that it was a front for his forging documents business, and I also knew that he got a fair share of his money from rich tourists who came here wanting to be the main actor in their very own porno movie. I know what you are thinking, this business is filled with creepy people, and yes, I agree. But the worst part is that there is a certain percentage of creepy people everywhere, and the dark web or the forgin business is no exception, nor is it a place where people or their interests are overrepresented. If 10% of the people on the dark web are into porn, then I would say that if you look around, every tenth person you see are into porn. We just don't tend to advertise with some parts of ourselves in public. In general. Then of course there are people who are open about just about every detail in their personal life. Completely erasing the border between personal information and private information.

Well, back to the story, I'm rambling again. Sorry. In the studio he took pictures of us, for drivers license and passports from America. One for a Bella Réal and one for a Sam Mercury. Close enough. He took us to an old house, where he said we could stay for the next few days, while he worked his magic and while attending his other business. The days passed quickly, and like that, we had new identities. We felt like secret agents on a mission. Bella identified another movie moment. Escape, his line of business and the way he had set up his work and studio, it was just like in a novel by Frederick Forsyth, that became a movie with Bruce Willis, the Jackal, but more like the book version than the movie version.

Except for cash, my friend wanted me to assist in some minor jobs that required me to use a computer, luckily, I did not need to do anything that would reveal my identity.

With our new identities, we could book regular airplane tickets to get to the United States of America. The land of opportunity.

Arriving in America

I didn't expect any trouble getting into America with our new identities, and the expectations were met. It is said that my former client is one of the best forgers there is. He even gets the identities in the national databases, sometimes with tax violations and all, for the authenticity of the identity created. But of course, not any current violations to not get in trouble. Just how he manages to do that, I've never asked. But in our case, it was clean sheets.

It was Bella that suggested where to go, Vegas. And I kind of understood where she was going with it... after all, I had popped the question, and she had said yes. Two times already. But it was still not a proper proposal, so I started thinking of how to do it, to get it just right.

Still inspired by the !y, we took local trains and buses and eventually got where we wanted to be. And wow! In the middle of nowhere. A city that never sleeps, with massive light shows in the dark and colorful arrangements everywhere at daytime. Like a digital 247/365 carnival in Rio. Mostly held indoors, but it spilled out on the streets as well.

We decided to keep a fairly low profile, and chose a cheaper hotel in the outskirts, cheaper not meaning cheap, only not ridiculously expensive. Not that we could not pay, but I wasn't comfortable in the high profile of the nicer and more famous hotels. Not to mention all the cameras.

The proposal

This time I wanted to get it right, third time's the charm, right?

We visited a jewelry store, one of many strange stores located within the hotel complexes. Even if I'd never thought I'd get married, this was important to me. Bella, a mission at first, became something greater and now, not someone I'd like to let go. Apparently we were not the only one's looking for wedding rings in Vegas. There was a vast number of rings to choose from in many different shapes and models, spanning from heavy diamond rings to simple and clean design, huge and heavy to small and light.

We settled for one ring each, from the same designer, Bella, a clean ring with a tiny diamond on top, discrete but there, sparkling as a diamond should when catching the surrounding light. As for me, a plain gold ring, no sparkling things, no patterns or details, just plain. Wide enough to feel robust, but thin enough not to take up the entire finger or being too much on the hand.

Once the rings were secured, it was finally time for the proposal. And when in Vegas, with my Bella, I could only think of one spot that would be a perfect spot for a proposal. The Bellagio fountain. I took her there in the sunset, to get the beauty of the setting sun, and to get the most out of the light-and water show.

I dropped down on one knee in front of her, with her ring between my fingers.

"Bella, my love, will you be my wife?"

"I do! So, so much!"

Then she went down on her knee, which surprised me.

"M3rqrie, will you be my partner?"

I got tears in my eyes, and could hardly answer her, it was so emotional, and I was not prepared for that. But I managed to get a reply across my lips.

"Yes! Yes! Yes!"

Then everything happened fast. I had not seen this kind of drive in Bella before, but she took me in her arms, then we got up together somehow, and got moving, and then, there was Elvis.

The Wedding

There is a certain magic about a proposal in Vegas. To some I guess it is a blessing, like for us, and for some it might not be. In our case, we, or rather Bella, found a chapel with Elvis performing the ceremony. Again, a movie moment, like the one by the fountain.

Now, weddings in Vegas are like an assembly line. To my surprise there was no fuss in the "husband and wife" or "wife and wife" part, we found "wife and partner" among the choices. To both our joy. Then it would truly be *our* wedding.

After Elvis did his thing, we did our "I do"-part, he pronounced us "partner and wife" and we kissed. As we kissed the air was filled with glittering confetti, worthy of Tinkerbell herself. Easily one of the happiest moments in my life!

We took a long walk in the Vegas nightlife, enjoying the moment, the night sky with a million stars shining on us, and for us. the chili but fresh air. Eventually our step led us back to our hotel and we fell asleep in eachothers arms, for the first time as partner and wife.

In the morning after at the breakfast table we had our first ever family meeting.

"Now that I have a wife, I'd like to leave everything behind me, start fresh somewhere, long way from technology, long way from N3v3r!and, shadow people, !y and whatever other fishes there might be in the big pond of this strange world."

"Me too, there is so much we have not had time to talk about just yet, but I long for somewhere peace and quiet where we can just be together, doing whatever we'd like with our time. No more running, no more hiding, just being, enjoying each other."

"I kind of feel bad for having dragged you into all this."

"Don't, my love. Please don't! I am happy to be here with you. I have nowhere else I'd rather be."

"But you work in London, friends, family?" Those were things we had not really covered yet.

"We'll get to that, but not now, not here. Let's just say that even though I liked my life in London, you changed everything for me. Now I just want to get away from it all to be somewhere with you. To be left alone, not worrying about getting kidnapped, not needing to look over our shoulders wondering who might be watching."

New life

"Where would you like to go?"

"Anywhere, perhaps somewhere in South America? Small town, near the ocean. We could have canteena, take care of stray dogs or work at an orphanage."

"That sounds nice, let's do that. Let's go to South America, find a nice town and settle down with something that feels meaningful."

"There is one more thing I'd like to do before we leave for our new life…"

"What's that, my love?"

"I'd like to go to New Orleans to enjoy the music."

"Then let's go there, perhaps catch a boat to the south. There are a lot of things I need to do as well."

"What, love?"

"Have you seen the movie Swordfish?"

"Yeah, I think so!"

"Then you know the hacker, played by Hugh Jackman, he hid code before he went to jail. I kind of need to do the same, there are some things I need to hide away, and even more that I need to delete and terminate."

"Then let's do that, and then we disappear."

"Yeah, the only problem is that as soon as I go online, I might trigger stuff that might give away our location."

"Then let's do it here, right now, and then we get the hell out of here!"

"Yeah, babe, I might need a day or two, but I'll be cautious. I don't want the place swarming with people who will be looking for us. Then I'll do as Jackman in Swordfish, and never return to the digital arena again. Even if he was sentenced to it, and I do it voluntarily."

Said and done. I got a set of devices that I needed, Bella started to work on our traveling path to New Orleans, and further.

Despite being in the middle of nowhere, in a desert, getting advanced and hightech gear in Vegas is not hard. They have very high and competent digital security, considering all the money that flows there.

Closing down a digital lifetime

Despite being a hacker, and used to cover my tracks, I had not ever planned on terminating my digital life's work. And I kind of had to solve things on the go, as I remembered things and figured out what else I needed to do.

Of course there were some things that I was determined to keep, and to keep safe, to prevent others from having it. Some things in the wrong hands can be devastating. In most of my work, I had created backdoors for me to use incase I ever needed. That information was important to keep to myself. So I set up storage areas in various places, clustered them into not containing any vital information, and distributed the things I needed to keep safe like a puzzle, leaving various pieces in various locations. The full picture only exists in my head, so no one else would be able to piece it together.

I also set up termination protocols, resembling the one's I had created for the N3v3r!and and !y. Only most of them were scheduled to execute once we were long gone settling in our new life.

Other stuff, I created boobietraps for intruders, so if someone were to snoop around, they would start chain reactions that would spread like an unstoppable domino. I felt proud of my work, I'd never thought I'd have the need to do it, and I had never given it any thought, but the three days I spent on setting it all up, I felt like I had created a really great setup, covering just about everything that needed to be covered.

If there remained any loose ends in the digital world, they would not matter, and they would not be able to be connected to anything, especially not after the termination protocol had started.

While I was busy with my things, Bella was busy on her end, and I was impressed by what she'd accomplished.

"First, I figured we'd make it more complicated for someone to follow us. We came here with our new identities. Should they be discovered, I'd figure we need to leave a trace leading away from here. So I've booked us airplane tickets for Washington DC. Then a few days later a flight from DC to New York. First class. Really expensive, but I think we are worth it! I'd like our honeymoon. From New York I suggest we travel !y-style down to New Orleans, and continue from there by boat as we talked about. Also, I've created mail-accounts for us, yours is Sam.Mercury@gmail.com, unfortunately, someone already uses Bella.Real@gmail.com, but Bella.Mercury@gmail.com was free, yay! Lucky me! And I've used those to get us into an online spanish-course, just to prepare us for what's coming."

Executing

I'd rigged everything I could possibly think of, and I'd been really careful in covering all my tracks as best as I could. Even so, as I executed the work, I was very nervous. The ideal would have hit the button and walked away. But I was a bit paranoid, and I wanted to make sure it got executed as intended. Took a good while for it all to run, but I did not see any hiccups nor that I'd triggered anything unusual.

Before leaving the hotel room, I put the computer in the microwave, and felt like Even, then we left for the airport and for our trip to Washington DC.

First class is something special, we had just about everything we'd wished for, in terms of foods and drinks, and entertainment. And we got to DC without any suspicious activity.
Felt like this would actually work, we could drop off the grid unnoticed. Start over. And you know what they say, time flies when you have a good time.

We had a fabulous time in DC. Real tourists but soon it was time for our flight to New York.

And when we arrived at the airport and checked in, we were shown to the fancy waiting lounge that was included in the first class tickets. There we had about an hour to kill before the flight was due.

A steward said that he would come for us once it was time to board the plane, which we would do just before take off, so we would not have to wait in uncomfortable lines or queues.

There were comfortable chairs and we had hot chocolate and played a few games of chess on a chessboard that were laying around along with various magazines and books.

I wondered how many that actually traveled in company with someone in first class, but perhaps there were more than I expected.

Eitherway, eventually we got called up to board our plane. Oh, and should I mention, Bella kicked my ass in chess, I had nothing on her.

Last chapter?

As Bella and I sat in the first class lounge on the airplane with a glass of champagne each, one of the stewards came to me with a sealed envelope with my name on it.

"M3rqrie"

It was odd, because nobody should know we were here, not N3v3r!and, not !y. Nobody, not even the broker. Besides, we were booked using our false identities, and nothing was connected to my name.

Bella just looked at me with a puzzled glance.

I shrugged my shoulders at her, and turned my attention to the envelope and opened it.

Inside was a phone. Felt like a scene in a movie. Surreal. But it was real.

The phone was powered on, and as I lifted it towards my face, the face recognition software activated and it opened up.

It was completely blank, not like any smartphone that I had seen before. There were just two icons. Text Messages and calls. Nothing else.

Suddenly, it vibrated in my hands and I got an incoming text.

I had to push the text message icon to open it.

"See you soon, M3rqrie!"

Nothing more.

Bella and I looked at each other.

The timestamp on the text indicated that someone had just sent it. But the sender was unknown.

Then they announced departure in the internal speaker system.

"Please fasten your seatbelts, we are about to take off. The duration of the flight is expected to be about ten hours, and we are scheduled to land in Reykjavik at 21.21 local time."

I met Bella's eyes, she looked a bit pale. Reykjavik? As in Iceland? Had we boarded the wrong plane? But if so, how was it that there was an envelope waiting for me?

"What do you think this is?" Bella asked me.

I shrugged my shoulders. " I have no idea, love!"

"Perhaps the past is catching up with us?" she said, and I felt that she was uneasy.